# ATHENA

## SIR PATRICK BIJOU

# PRELUDE

*When one assignment turns out to be more than she can chew, Athena's job as a journalist may very well lead to her own undoing.*

Tree branches loom over Athena, casting dark shadows on the path toward the infamous Sarton Asylum. Then and there she gets a bad feeling about the place, but a job is a job.

She needs the money and her morbid curiosity always gets the best of her.

As soon as she nears the asylum's doors, her hand shakes. A signal for what's to come perhaps? Or just her nerves?

Regardless, it doesn't take a believer to convince Athena that taking this assignment is a mistake. Slowly, she uncovers the stomach-churning horrors that were inflicted upon Sarton's residents.

*"Why would anyone do any of these experiments, especially on children? How did any of that get approved by any doctor?"*, she thinks to herself. Now, all she wants to do is head back home to her brother, Derek, and her dog, Ginger.

But her thoughts get interrupted by a disturbing presence.

In all her years as a journalist investigating haunted buildings, nothing like this has ever happened to her. None of those buildings were ever haunted. They were all shams, for the lack of a better word. Unfortunately for Athena – this time – the Sarton Asylum could very well be the last assignment she'll ever have to take.

Enter a world of terror and chaos where victims are left helpless and tortured beyond their understanding in the gripping paranormal novel, **"Athena"**.

*Will they find a way to survive, or will they succumb to the horrors that lie ahead?*

# ABOUT THE AUTHOR

Sir Patrick Bijou lives and writes from the United Kingdom and is the author of several books on finance and fiction. He is known for his extraordinary skills in settling and negotiating peace settlements and international law and is a prodigious legal and political adviser. His diverse writing ability has been influenced by many experiences, making him the success he is today.

Sir Patrick has written many books and articles about the liberation of people, highlighting the issues of those whom the literary world of creative writing has not enlightened. His expedition into content writing has made him a remarkably inspired author and professional communicator.

He has written over 32 non-fictional and fictional books spanning different genres.

Finding his Books.

To find out more about Sir Patrick, visit his website.

www.sirpatrickbijou.com
www.bijouebook.com

A thena Pierce woke up and outstretched her
arms. She reached for her glasses, got out of
bed, and walked to her window, opening the blinds.
She gazed out at the large lake outside and sighed.
"Maybe I can go deeper today?" she spoke to her dog,
Ginger, who was lying on the bed wagging her tail.

Ginger was a small cairn terrier with bright blue
eyes. Her long coat was the color of wheat. She was
looking at Athena with love and curiosity. Her
brother had always teased her by naming her dog
Ginger when she wasn't close to the same color as
the name. Athena didn't care. She had named her
after her favorite character on Gilligan's Island,
Ginger Grant. She and her brother used to watch that
show after school while waiting for their mother to
return home from work.

Athena loved adventure. Recently, her activities
had included diving into the large lake outside and
seeing how far she could go before she needed to
take a breath. She turned to her dog and ruffled the
fur on her head as she walked into the bathroom. She
stopped at the sink and looked at her reflection in
the mirror. Her shoulder-length blond hair stuck up
everywhere. The bags underneath her blue eyes
indicated that she hadn't slept as well as she had
thought she did. She sighed as she turned the
showerhead on and undressed.

She had always been adventurous. When she
was little, her mother used to panic that Athena
would run off somewhere and get taken. At the time,
she thought her mother was being ridiculous, but

now she understood what her mother was thinking. She had written too many articles about children being taken away from their parents.

After taking a shower, she wrapped herself in a towel and walked to her dresser. She took out a pair of skinny jeans and an old blue t-shirt. She got dressed and combed through her hair, pulling it into a loose braid. She wasn't a fan of keeping her hair long, but she kept it this way for her mother. She had the same hair as her mother, and it was the only thing she had left to remember her by. Her mother had died a couple of years ago. The doctors didn't understand why she had passed away; they still didn't know. She shifted her glasses back onto her face and walked down the stairs on her way to the kitchen.

She fed Ginger and started to fix breakfast for herself. While she began mixing the pancake mix, the kitchen phone rang. Athena reached over and took the phone off the receiver, holding it between her ear and shoulder, and continued mixing.

"Hello?" she asked politely into the phone.

"Miss Athena?" the voice on the other end perked up. Hi!"

Athena smiled at the familiar, graveled voice. "Mr. Schneider?" Mr. Schneider was the head reporter of the Sarton Paper and her boss. Whenever there was a place that he needed a piece written on, he handed it over to Athena. Mr. Schneider was the man who gave her her first job when she graduated college four years ago. Now, only being twenty- six, she had become the best reporter at the Sarton Paper

Company. She enjoyed her job and was very grateful for Mr. Schneider's encouragement.

"I think you're going to like this one," he excitedly told her. "It's right up to your speed."

"What's it about?" She dropped the wooden spoon she held onto the ground, causing pancake mix to splatter on the floor. "Damn it," she muttered under her breath, hoping Mr. Schneider didn't hear her cussing.

A slight laugh came from the other end. Athena smiled and winced slightly as that laugh showed that he had indeed heard her cuss. "For years, I have been trying to get permission for someone to go check out the Sarton Asylum, and now I've settled it! I would like it if you would go and check it out for me."

She had picked up the spoon and stopped short of putting it back into the bowl. "You mean the abandoned Sarton Asylum?" she asked as she shuffled over to the sink to wash the spoon.

"Yes, that's right." His voice still held the cheeriness from his victory.

"They say that place is haunted, Mr. Schneider," Athena mentioned slowly.

She could almost see him shrugging his shoulders as he responded, "That hasn't stopped you before." He paused, letting that sink in. "So, what do you think? Will you do it?"

He told the truth. Athena had been in a haunted house before, but nothing happened to her while she stayed there. It turned out to be a rumor and not exciting. Athena chewed on her lip, thinking about it for a minute or two before answering, "Sure. I'll do it." Rumors are only rumors, after all, she thought.

"Good. I'll send you the directions to the asylum through e-mail. Talk to you soon, Miss Athena." Mr. Schneider was still in the age of e-mails. She had mentioned to him before about sending directions through text messages, but he never could remember to do it. It was easier for him to do e-mails, so she let it be. She had eventually given up on reminding him and had gotten used to it. It didn't matter anyway; it was still a good form of communication.

"Thank you, Mr. Schneider. Goodbye." She hung up the phone and placed it back on the receiver. After washing the spoon, she continued cooking, thinking about Sarton Asylum the whole time. No one had gone into that building for decades. The only person who had, about ten years ago, never came out. People believed that he died there and possibly he had. They were never able to find a body when searchers went in for him. Athena shuddered, placed saran wrap over the bowl, and then placed it in the refrigerator. I've lost my appetite, she thought.

She almost thought about telling Mr. Schneider that she had changed her mind about going. She had a feeling that something was going to happen, but she had thought about that before on other assignments, and nothing happened.

Ginger whined at her feet and nudged them with her nose.

Athena looked down at Ginger and gave her an apologetic smile. "I'm sorry, girl." She patted her leg. "Come on, I'll let you out." She walked outside and watched Ginger run around the backyard. Inside, she heard a beep come from her computer. She walked back inside, knowing that Ginger would be safe in her fenced-in yard, and opened her e-mail.

The e-mail held directions to Sarton Asylum, and Athena took out her iPhone and punched in the directions Mr. Schneider had given her through the e-mail. Ginger scratched at the door, and Athena jumped up to let her in before walking back to her computer.

"Looks like he wants me to go today," she told her dog. "I'll text Derek so he can take care of you." She scratched between Gingers' ears as she texted her brother and then went upstairs to pack.

Thirty minutes later, Athena found herself standing at the front door with her small suitcase on the ground. She never knew how long she would be gone whenever she went on her assignments, but she always took a couple of pairs of clothes and essentials in case it was a longer trip. A knock came from the other side of the door. She opened it to see her brother, Derek, standing there with a duffle bag slung over his shoulder. He knew the drill as much as she did.

Derek was her younger brother by five years. He had the same blond hair and blue eyes as she did. He had just got done with college and started working at the Sarton Paper as an assistant for Mr. Schneider. Right now, he just fetches coffee and organizes papers in the office, but he is a good writer. Soon he'll be able to go out on assignments.

"Hi, Derek," she greeted as she greeted her brother. She ushered him in and gave him a piece of paper with what to do for Ginger.

"Sis," Derek groaned but took the paper anyway, "I've done this about a thousand times. Come on, don't you trust me to remember how to take care of Ginger?"

Athena rolled her eyes as she brought him in for a quick hug. "Yes, I trust you. If I didn't, you wouldn't be here caring for my baby." She reached down and patted Ginger's head. "Goodbye, Ginger." She looked back up at her brother. "Take care, Derek. See you both soon."

"Bye, sis!"

Athena nodded as she grabbed her suitcase and walked past them. She walked out the door and over to her car. She put the suitcase in the trunk before climbing into the driver's seat. Starting the car, she looked up and saw Derek standing at the door with Ginger by his side. I'll be back soon, she told herself. Backing out of the driveway, she headed toward Sarton Asylum.

Athena drove for about thirty minutes until she came to a large brick sign. It read Sarton Asylum in bold golden letters, some of the letters chipping, brown, and ready to fall off at any time. The sign signified how old it truly is. Once used to be white brick now looked green and brown from the moss and dirt caked onto it from years of neglect. A large gate blocked Athena's entrance to the asylum.

"Creepy," she whispered to herself. The sight of the old sign was creepy to her; she still admired the beauty that time gave to it. Helped show character to the asylum.

She parked the car in front of the gate and got out before walking up to it. There she noticed it didn't have a lock. Pushing on the heavy gate, Athena finally got it opened wide enough for her car to go through. Walking back to her car and climbing in, she put it in drive and drove down the long driveway lined with tall trees. Their thick branches loomed over the path, making it look like it was dark outside, while it was only the middle of the day. The thick branches blocked any kind of light from flowing through.

Little ways down the driveway, the music from her radio started to fizzle out. Annoyed by it, she reached over and tried to turn the radio down, but it wouldn't comply. Giving up, she tried to ignore the static and instead focused on the dirt road. The branches must be blocking the satellite from reaching my radio, she thought to herself. While it annoyed her, it didn't seem like anything could be wrong. But a few seconds later, Athena heard something come from the radio.

"Bzzzzzzzz...turn...bzzzzzzzz...go...bzzzzzzzz..."

Athena stopped the car and looked at the radio, her eyebrows furrowing. That didn't sound like a song, she thought. That voice wasn't singing. "Turn!...bzzzzz...go!...bzzzzz...now!....bzzzzz..."

Suddenly, the radio stopped fizzling, and the music continued as before. Athena shook her head, clearing her thoughts, and continued driving. She assumed the radio had initially not picked up the satellite signal. She'd been through situations like this in the past. For the most part, they were annoying hackers who thought it to be funny to mess with her radio. As she learned in the past, she ignored it.

As she kept driving, Athena took note of her surroundings. The leaves of the trees were brown and red from the changing weather, and the tree bark looked dark and rough. The dirt-covered driveway had leaves littering that fell from the trees above. The trees blocked the view of the sun, making the driveway dark and eerie.

Finally, Athena rolled up to the asylum. Goosebumps traveled over her body. She got a good look at the large, red-bricked building. While the red may have once been bright and beautiful, it now started to fade and become ugly. There were many windows spaced out along the building, with some of them broken in places. Above the large, black door, thin, rusty letters read Sarton Asylum. Vines covered one side of the building; bushes were overgrown, and dead flowers lined the path up to the entrance. At least, she thought they were flowers. They were too shriveled up and black.

"Wow," Athena breathed as she stopped the car. She got out of the car, taking her phone out to take a picture of the asylum. "Mr. Schneider would love to see this." She sent him the photo via email, then took another good look at the photo. "It's even creepier in a picture." Athena chuckled, then paused. "Wait— what's that?" She looked closer, and her eyes widened. In the image, a black-haired girl in a white nightgown stood in the far right window on the second story. Athena looked up at that same window but saw no one. She stood there watching for a while, hoping to see the girl, but she never returned. Now I'm starting to see things, she thought. Great.

She held up her phone, looking at the picture again. Her eyebrows furrowed as she saw the little girl in the picture, but she wasn't there when she looked up at the same window. She started feeling weird about this assignment, but she shook her head. She needed the money, and besides, she loved the adventure.

Athena closed her eyes, trying to clear the image of the girl from her mind. Breathing out, she opened her eyes and looked down at her watch. Three o'clock. "I'll only stay till six," she told herself. "Then I'll go home and rest before coming back tomorrow. I'm not staying here. "The reporter locked her car and walked towards the door, slowing down as she came closer. She stopped once she got there, and her hand started to shake while reaching for the doorknob. Composing herself, she opened the door and stepped inside. Yes, the asylum was creepy, but she should be able to compose herself in these situations. She's been in others like this assignment before and wasn't afraid. Her mind and body were trying to tell her something, but she couldn't understand what it was.

The air stunk of mildew and mold, and she held her breath. She covered her nose with her sleeve as she ventured in and took a look around. She saw the opening of a long hallway, and as she continued to walk down to the other end, it led to a large staircase. The walls had various sizes of cracks, and pictures were either crooked or on the floor in pieces. Underneath her feet, the rug had brown stains and was ripped in many places. With a bit of fumbling, Athena found a light switch by the door and flipped it on. Nothing. Damn it. Taking out her phone, she turned on the flashlight and shone its light in front of her as she walked forward. She passed the first door on her right and turned her flashlight on it.

The door was made from aged oak wood and had a gold plate stuck on it that, upon closer inspection, read The InterviewRoom: Ms. Parrish. The golden plate had a thick coat of dust on it. Athena grabbed the handle and opened the door. Inside, the room happened to be about the size of an average office. It had a large desk on the left side of the room and a large brown chair with many holes behind it. Two chairs were overturned and were on opposite sides of the room. Books and papers were scattered across the floor, and pictures hung off-centered from the walls.

Athena walked around the room and noticed an old-looking radio sitting on top of a table covered in dust. She bent down to look at the small plate on the radio. 1920. She straightened slowly and turned to walk away—but then radio static filled the room.

"Bzzzzzzz...I gave you a warning...bzzzzz...I gave you a warning..."

Athena spun around, her heart pounding in her chest. Her breathing quickened; the voice sounded like a child's. A little girl.

"Bzzzzzzzzz...I gave you a warning...bzzzzzzzzz...why didn't you listen?" The static distorted a horrible cackle, making the hair on Athena's neck stand up. The radio fizzled again, then turned off and became silent.

Athena stood there staring at the radio. She couldn't believe her ears. A girl's voice—a young girl's voice—came out of the radio. Nothing in this building worked; the electricity had been cut off decades ago. So how could the radio turn on? She tried flipping the switch, but nothing happened. Athena closed her eyes and took deep breaths, counting to ten, calming herself down.

It's like the girl in the window. What if I just imagined it? It could also be whoever messed with my radio signal.

Giving the radio one last look, Athena quickly left the room and continued to explore the rest of the building. The incident with the radio soon left her mind because nothing strange had happened in the other rooms downstairs.

Nothing yet, anyway.

A few hours later, Athena stood at the bottom of the stairs at the end of the hallway. She had already been through the other rooms and found that each happened to be the same as the first. Each of them held interview rooms designed for each new member of the asylum. They had held the children's names on a golden, dust-covered plaque on the desks. As it occurred in the first room before, everything in the room was a mess. Books and papers were thrown all over the floor, chairs were turned over, and the big chairs were filled with holes.

Everything appeared the same except the radio. Each room had a radio, but they were all broken and lying in the corner of the room. The only radio that wasn't broken happened to be the one in the first room. Every time she saw a broken radio, Athena wondered, Why would this one be broken and the first one not be? She didn't know and didn't want to stick around long enough in each room to find out. She had quickly gone over everything in the room, making notes of what was in it before sprinting out.

Athena looked through the books that were still together and sat on the bookshelves in each room. Each book talked about the insane and how to treat them. There were all kinds of ways to treat them. She didn't know there were so many different ways to provide treatment to them. The ones on the shelves were more humane and talked about ways to talk to them about their problems. Then when she looked at the pages and books torn apart on the floor, sadly, she noticed something completely different. These books were also on how to treat the insane but in torturous ways. Each room had the same kind of books. Each time Athena read the ones on the floor, she felt sick to her stomach. Finally, she had enough of reading the books and threw the one she held across the room. She then stood up and stormed out of the room, where she came to stand in front of the stairs.

Athena couldn't understand why anyone would do any of those experiments on anyone. Especially children. How did any of that get approved by any doctor? She clenched her fists as she stood in front of the massive staircase.

She shined her flashlight up the staircase and back down to her feet. The staircase was made of old wood, and the same carpet as the floor ran up to the middle of the stairs, creating a runway.

She touched the handle and smiled wistfully. This must have been a beautiful staircase, she thought to herself. She then felt the hairs on the back of her neck stand up as a creepy feeling as if someone was watching her. Slowly, she lifted the flashlight to the stairs and gasped when it landed on a little girl.

She looked exactly like the girl she had seen in the outside window. Her white dress had brown and green stains over it, and her long black hair hung over her eyes; all Athena saw of her face were her nose and mouth. Her skin looked dirty and bruised.

Athena stood there with her mouth gaping wide at the girl. She didn't know what to do. Should she try speaking to the girl? Should she ignore her and try walking up the stairs past her? Or should she run? Athena didn't know what to do, and time seemed to freeze. The air around her turned cold, and goosebumps raised on her skin. Never before had she encountered someone in her assignments of abandoned places. Sure, she had taken people to them but never met someone. She had once taken her brother on one of her assignments when he was still thinking about going into a journalism career.

Finally, she decided it was time to make a decision. She opened her mouth and asked the girl, "H-hello?" Athena was startled when she noticed fog coming from her mouth. She wrapped an arm around her while she kept her phone's lit up at the girl. She started to shake from the sudden temperature drop.

The little girl just stared at her, or so Athena thought, since she couldn't see her eyes. She remained silent. Athena wished that she would say something. Although, she was still hoping that she was hallucinating and dreaming. Perhaps she would wake up and still be at home.

"What's your name?" Athena tried again. She couldn't stop her body from shaking.

The girl raised her hand and pointed to Athena's hand resting on the rail. Athena slowly looked over and, reluctantly, shined her light where her hand used to be. A name was etched into the wood, Effie. Was that her name?

"Effie," Athena read aloud; her teeth were now chattering. "Is that your name?" She shined her light on the top of the stairs, but the girl wasn't there anymore. The temperature fluctuated quickly. It started to go back to normal until it dropped drastically again. Athena then felt a presence to her right. She whipped her body to the right and turned the flashlight there to see the girl standing beside her looking at her. The girl's hair was parted slightly, showing her glowing, yellow eyes looking right at Athena. Athena yelped and jumped back, hitting her back on the opposite railing.

The girl nodded her head, finally answering Athena's question. "I warned you." The voice was high, like a child's, but it came out slow and creepy. "I warned you to get out." Athena registered that this was the same voice that she had heard through the radio and her car's radio. The girl cocked her head to one side. "Why didn't you listen to me?" Her mouth was turned down in a worried expression.

Not expecting her to speak, Athena stood there opening and closing her mouth, not knowing what to say. "Well, I-I," she stammered. Her body was shaking uncontrollably either from the cold air or the fear that was starting to go through her body. She couldn't tell which it was.

Suddenly, the ends of the girl's hair started to stand up. Her eyes started to glow even brighter. "Get out!" the girl screamed. Her mouth opened wide, causing her jaw to dislocate, and a strong gust of wind came out that knocked Athena off her feet and slammed her into the wall behind her. A sharp pain went through her as she hit the wall and crumbled to the floor.

Athena's phone flew out of her hand, landing on the floor a little away. She went to grab it and shined the light where the girl once was. She was gone again. Athena now took the girl's advice and ran down the hallway and tried to get out the door, but it wouldn't budge. Her body screamed in pain, but she didn't care. She wanted to get out. She needed to get out.

"No!" Athena yelled, not caring if the girl could hear her or not. She banged her fists against the door several times and tugged on the handle before giving up and trying to find another way out. She knew that her hands were going to have bruises on them, but again, she didn't care. She quickly checked her phone and cursed when she saw that she didn't have any service.

She decided to run into the first room. She searched through it and ran to the window. She tried opening it, but it wouldn't budge either. Panicking, Athena looked around for something to throw at the window to break it. She saw a small chair sitting in one corner and went to grab it. When she got there and picked it up, she felt something hard slam against the back of her head. She dropped the chair and collapsed onto the floor; her vision started to blacken. The last thing she saw was the radio and a pair of small dirty feet standing in front of her.

"I warned you," the girl's voice sang out again. Then Athena blacked out.

Athena woke up on the ground with a severe headache. She sat up slowly, holding her head with one of her hands, and looked around the room. A single lamp in the middle of the room let off a soft circle of light. The circle of light stretched just a few feet in front of Athena. She couldn't see what the rest of the room looked like since it stayed pitch black where the light didn't touch.

Athena's heart started racing when the memories of earlier that day returned to her. The little girl hit her with the radio! It seemed as if she didn't want Athena to leave, but she kept telling her to get out.

At least, she thought that it was earlier that day. She didn't know how long she had been lying here passed out. Her whole body was aching. She was in so much pain.

A sound came from behind her, and Athena scrambled over to the circle of light. She hoped the light would protect her. She gripped the leg of the lamp and looked around her, trying to find whatever or whoever made that sound.

Was that the little girl? she asked herself. What did she say her name was? Her mind was fuzzy.

A child's laughter filled the room. The air around Athena turned cold once again. She wrapped her arms around herself, and a girl's high voice came from the other side, "My name was Effie." The sudden temperature drop caused her to start shaking, making pain shoot through her body.

Athena turned toward the voice. "E-Effie? Was?" Her breath came out in a fog.

The laughter came again. This time, it sounded like it was exactly behind Athena. She turned around but saw no one. "That's right," the girl firmly told her. "Effie was my name. I was the last child to stay in this miserable hell hole!" Her voice echoed around Athena. Her voice made it impossible to know which direction she was talking from. "I wanted to escape for so long, but I couldn't. I became trapped and tortured." She laughed maniacally. "I was never insane! They thought I was, but I wasn't! Those idiots ruined me." There was a slight pause before her voice sounded close to Athena's ear, "Do you know what electricity flowing through your head feels like?"

The hairs on Athena's arms stood up. Athena felt a presence extremely close behind her. The air around her started to feel static. Something shocked the back of her neck, making her jump and turn around.

She turned in a circle searching for Effie. "What happened to you?" All at once, everything became silent. Athena turned around in a circle again, but she found no one like all the times before. Athena couldn't see anything through the pitch-black. She didn't even know that a room could get that dark. She opened her mouth to ask the question again when the overhead lights came on over her head. She shielded her eyes so they could get used to the white, bright light.

Once her eyes adjusted to the white light, she looked around her. It was a white, windowless room. There was no way to figure out what time of day it was outside. There was a single gray dentist chair against one wall with a metal table beside it. The chair had many holes in it and what looked like old red stains all over. She walked over to the chair and noticed many claw marks dug into the chair. Leather straps hung over the sides, torn. The air around her had suddenly turned warm.

Athena's knees were weak as she turned around but saw nothing else or no one else in the room. She took a deep breath, held her head high, balled up her fists, and yelled, "Where are you?" She waited for an answer she knew wouldn't come. Pointing to the chair, she called out again, "Why did you show me this?" She needed answers. She needed Effie to keep talking to her. Athena figured if she could keep her talking, she could prevent whatever Effie wanted to do to her. She could even figure out how to get out of there and head back home where it was safe. She knew that she wasn't safe here.

The temperature in the room dropped drastically. Athena wrapped her arms around her and ran her hands up and down her arms, trying to get some warmth. All of a sudden, she saw something shiny flying through the air toward her. She screamed and ducked just in time as the object flew through the space where her head had been just seconds before. She shakily turned to see a rusty knife sticking out of the wall behind the chair.

"I wouldn't yell at me if I were you," the little girl's chilling, sharp voice came from nowhere.

"That's what the idiots did, and it didn't end well for them."

Still squatting on the floor, Athena slowly asked the girl, "W-what do you mean? What d- did they do to you?" She looked over her shoulder and at the knife, and her eyes widened. "What did you d-do to them?" her voice squeaked. She needed to keep her talking. She urged Effie to keep talking to her. The longer she was in here, maybe she could get some more information that would help her help the girl.

"P-please, Effie," Athena urged. "Talk to me." She started to stand up slowly. She tried to keep control over her body and stop it from shaking.

"Why would you want to know anything?" She heard Effie sneer somewhere in the room. "You read the books downstairs. You know exactly what they did to me." Athena heard a loud huff somewhere behind her.

Athena nodded slowly. "T-then tell me what you did to the doctors who did t-this to you." There was silence. The air around her was still cold. She could still see the fog coming out of her mouth and nose.

Suddenly, a horrible, shrilled laugh filled the air, making Athena cover her ears and put her head between her knees. "You'll see." Then, the only door in the room slammed shut.

Athena screamed and ran over to the door, trying to open it. She tugged on the handle of the door and continuously slammed her shoulder against it until it was bruised. "No, no, no!" It was locked. She leaned against the door and slid down. She wrapped her arms around her knees and began to cry. She became trapped.

"Effie!"

Athena sat on the floor for a couple more minutes before standing up and trying to tug on the door handle again. Her body was trying to shut down. Her body was in too much pain. Every inch that she moved was agonizing. She tried to open the door, but no matter how hard she shook and pulled the door handle, it would not budge. She remained locked in here with no way to escape. There was no way to tell what time it was. No way to tell if it could be night or day. There were no windows in the room to tell her whether it was night or day.

Remembering her phone in her pocket, she whipped it out. She thanked whoever was listening to her that it was still working and turned it on. She tried to text her brother but noticed that she didn't have service. Her text wouldn't send. "Damn it!" She frustratedly hit the send button a dozen times before giving up. She roughly stuffed her phone back into her pocket.

She turned around and looked around the room, desperate to find anything that could open the door. She ran over to the table by the chair and took the gray, rusty tray off of it. Running back to the door, she tried to place the tray between the door and the wall but failed. It was just too big.

"Damn it!" she screamed again, throwing the tray on the ground. It made a loud clattering noise until it lay still. She needed to calm down and make a rational decision.

She turned back around and threw her hands down in frustration. She closed her eyes and took some deep breaths before opening them again. She then remembered the knife sticking out of the wall and ran over to it. She struggled a little to pull it out of the wall, but finally, it came out. She stumbled back a little and hit the back of her knees against the chair, causing her to sit down hard against it. She had a light vision of her being strapped to the chair and an electrical poker against her temple. Her breath caught in her throat as she felt electricity pulsating through her body. She screamed and tried to get out of the restraints that had snaked up around her body. Electrifying pain shot up and down her body before she was pulled back into reality.

She shook the vision out of her head. She sat there for a few minutes, gathering her breath before running back to the door. She tried to slide the knife in between the door handle and the wall. Wiggling the knife back and forth and up and down. Athena started to pray to anyone who was listening that this would work. That she would be able to be free.

Finally, to her surprise, she heard a small click. She pulled the knife out and slowly reached for the knob. Her hand shook as it turned, and she pushed it open. The hallway outside had a large window at one end with its blinds opened to reveal a bright, yellow morning light.

She reluctantly stuck her head out of the doorway and looked up and down the hall. Seeing no one, she held the knife out in front of her and turned toward the stairs. A knife wasn't going to do anything against Effie, but it gave Athena slight comfort. She looked down the stairway—no one again. Looking beside her, she saw a door propped open.

Curiosity killed the cat. I'm not the cat today, she prayed with hope. Athena had always been curious about everything. Her mother had once called her too curious. That is why she joined the paper and became a reporter. She got to be curious without anyone telling her not to be also, she got paid. Please, let me not be the cat. Oh, why do I have to be the curious cat?

When she was a young girl, she would get in all sorts of trouble for being curious. Mixed with her love for adventure, she would always venture too far from the house. Her mother was always a mess whenever she walked too far. Her mother had resorted to making rules and putting locks on the door that she couldn't reach until her brother was big enough to protect her.

That wasn't long. Athena wasn't a tall woman; she was mostly average. Her brother was able to shoot up above her by the time he was thirteen. Then, her mother was not as reluctant to let Athena walk away from the house.

After working on the paper, Athena understood why she was so cautious about letting her daughter out of her sight when she was extremely young and frail.

Walking to the door, she nudged it open and held the knife in front of her. The knife shook violently in her hands. The room looked like a bedroom for a young child. By any means, a little girl from the amount of dusty, torn stuffed animals laid on and around the bed. A twin bed sat against the opposite wall, and a dresser was on the right wall. A dirty red, round rug sat in the middle of the room. She walked over to one wall and gasped at all the pictures that were hanging.

"Is she Effie?" she asked in a low voice while staring at a young girl standing in front of the asylum. She sure looked like the scary child that wouldn't leave Athena alone. The little girl had clean black hair running with no effort down her back. In the picture, she wore a beautiful white dress that ran down to the middle of her shins and puffy sleeves. Her smile was beautiful and full of happiness.

What happened to her?

Athena slowly let the knife drop by her side. She smiled sadly at the picture. "The poor girl," she whispered. She touched the picture, and a sound behind her made her jump. She whirled around with the knife held out in front of her again. There was no one there. She growled in anger and yelled, "What do you want?" She held her arms out beside her. "Why did you lock me in that room? What do you want from me?" She waited for an answer but got none. "I wasn't the one that hurt you!"

Athena started to shake when she noticed that the room got cold, and she could see her breath coming out of her nose and mouth.

A peal of cold laughter filled the air. Athena's breath quickened. The pictures behind Athena started to shake and fly off the wall. Athena ducked as one came straight for her head. The picture shattered as it hit the opposite wall and fell to the ground. Athena saw movements in one corner and looked over to see the little girl standing in the dark, her glowing yellow eyes staring straight at her.

"What do you want from me?" Athena asked slowly, irritated. The knife she held in front of her started shaking even more violently.

The little girl smiled menacingly. "I want you to suffer as I did!" She held a syringe full of clear liquid in her hand and came toward Athena. Some form of thick, red liquid came out of her mouth. Athena automatically thought that it was blood.

Athena held out the knife in front of her for protection. "Stay away, or I swear I will use this!" She was trying to control her voice from shaking, but she couldn't control her body spasming.

The girl laughed and kept coming at her. "You're just like them, aren't you? An idiot. Do you think a rusty old knife will help you against me? Ha! Guess what? I'm dead!" The girl jumped toward Athena but jumped out of the way and ran for the door.

She slammed the door closed behind her and ran down the staircase. Running down the hallway, she came upon the front door. To her surprise, it opened. She ran outside to her car and grabbed the keys. Putting the keys into the ignition and turning them, she heard an odd sound coming out from the engine.

"No, no, no!" she screamed. "Please start! Please start!" Tears started to stream down her cheeks. She looked up to see the little girl standing in the same second-story window as before. The girl shook her head, smirked, and disappeared. Athena tried to jump-start her car but to no avail. She ended up giving up and got out of the car. She wrapped her arms around her and shivered. "It only took thirty minutes to get here." She looked back at the house. "I'll be back for my car. I can't stay here."

She started to walk in the direction of the gate. The sun was starting to set over the building causing a looming shadow. Athena kept trying not to look back at the building but couldn't help herself. She felt like she was being watched intently. She thought that she could hear movement on either side of her.

She finally stepped onto the long driveway and kept her focus on the gate at the end. The trees seemed to stretch over her more this time. She clenched her jaw as she started to imagine the trees grabbing her and throwing her back into the house. Athena quickened her pace after that thought.

The dark movement came from the corner of her eye, causing her to jump. She snapped her head over to that side but saw nothing. She started to jog towards the gate. Her brows furrowed as she noticed she hadn't gotten closer to the gate. She was still the same distance as she was when she first started walking. She started to sprint towards the gate, and tears came to her eyes again as she confirmed what she feared. The gate wasn't getting closer.

Athena screamed as she tripped over a root and fell face-first into the dirt. When she finally looked up, she was in front of the dark door of the asylum. Tears fell down her face as the door creaked open, and a pair of hands grabbed her and pulled her into the asylum. Athena lay in the fetal position on the dirty, dingy carpet. She felt defeated. She wanted to go home but knew that wasn't a chance. She would have to figure out a way to get out of this asylum alive. There was nowhere else for her to go. She slowly stood up and dusted the dirt off of her shirt and pants. She would have to figure out how to survive here until her brother came and got her.

She hoped her brother would eventually figure out that something was wrong. She just hoped that it wouldn't be too late.

Athena needed to figure out how to help Effie. If she could figure out what exactly they did to her and then what she did to them, maybe she could figure out how to put her soul at ease. There had to be a different way than getting revenge on Athena. She wasn't ready to die.

She grabbed her phone out of her pocket and hoped for some form of reception. None. She sighed and looked at how much life she had left.

"Thirty percent," she sighed again. She turned around and noticed little bloody handprints covering the door. They were small, childlike hands all over the door. She instantly knew that those hands were Effie's. She shivered and turned back around. She pushed the image of the handprints out of her head and held her hands up in surrender, hoping that this would only work a little. She needed rest. "All right. Listen, Effie, I'm not going to hurt you; I can't. I just want to go home, so please, let me go home. I'll never return. I promise." She waited to see if she would get a response, but she never did. Athena thought that maybe she would get a response from her. Effie had been tormenting her all day, but now nothing. Athena pushed down the silly thought that ghosts had to rest just like she did.

Athena shook her head as she put her hands down and walked into the first room to her right. She looked around the room and found a blanket in a closet that wasn't eaten by moths and a couple of seat cushions without holes in them on the floor. She cleaned off a section of the floor and laid down. She placed the cushions behind her head comfortably and the blanket over her. She decided that she was going to wait out and wait for her brother to come and get her. Eventually, he'll figure out that she's been gone longer than usual without any contact and will come to look for her.

Athena looked around the room and noticed the radio that she had contact with earlier that day. She instantly got up and picked up the radio. She placed it outside of the room before she returned to her blanket.

Staring up at the ceiling, she wondered why this little girl was still there. Athena knew that she was dead, but why would she continue to stay and haunt this place? She shook her head as her curiosity got better and decided that she had to have answers.

Athena threw the blanket off of her and walked around the room. She opened drawers and cabinets, trying to find some clue as to why this girl was still there. After looking through every single hiding space, she found nothing. She then remembered the room with all the pictures. The room that had belonged to Effie.

Taking out her phone, she turned the flashlight on. She walked out of the room, down the hallway, and up the stairs. She then turned to her left and walked into what used to be Effie's room. She turned her flashlight toward the pictures and walked over to them. She shivered as she noticed that all of the pictures were now back up on the wall as if they weren't thrown at her earlier.

The first picture she saw was the same one as before. Effie was standing in front of the asylum with a large smile on her face. She looked happy. Perhaps she was placed here for her own well-being and wasn't supposed to be here long. Walking to the right, she looked at the many pictures of Effie in this room. Each picture appeared the same, but the only difference was in her smile. In each picture, her smile would become smaller and smaller until it finally became just a frown. Her eyes were filled with hatred.

Athena touched the last picture and sighed sadly. "This poor girl," she whispered to herself. She looked closer at the picture and saw a figure standing behind Effie. "Who is that?"

The figure looked like an old lady with her hair hanging over her eyes and a long black dress torn in places. She looked to be transparent, like a ghost.

Athena touched the picture where the transparent woman stood and heard a crack below her. She looked down to see the wooden floor breaking beneath her feet. She turned in haste, ready to run. The floor gave out, and she fell through the hole and landed on the wood from the room underneath.

Groaning, Athena slowly sat up when a crack sounded again underneath.

"Oh, no," she whispered. She screamed as she fell through the new hole and landed on the hard concrete floor. She grimaced as she placed her hand on the back of her head and felt something wet. She looked at her hand to see blood smeared across it. She slowly, shaking, sat up and looked around her, noticing that she was lying in the basement. Her whole body was in agonizing pain. Her legs were hurting the most, but she needed to get up. If she just lay here, who knows what would happen to her.

There wasn't much in the basement, just a few boxes and old, broken toys. It was too dark and damp, and the air smelled like mildew. There was a large hole in the middle of the basement floor.

Athena slowly stood up, limped over to the hole, and looked down. Stars danced in her vision, and she blinked, trying to make them disappear. The hole was square and about the size of a child. Athena gasped when she saw dirty stuffed animals and broken toys lying in the hole.

Why would a hole be put down here? She asked herself. The air turned cold around her, and she heard heavy breathing come from behind her. She turned around to find Effie standing right behind her.

Athena looked down into Effie's lifeless face. Her breathing became heavier, and her heartbeat began to increase. She placed her hands up and tried to sidestep Effie, but Effie mirrored her moves, blocking her.

"What do you want?" Athena asked her. Her voice quivered with fear.

Effie stared at her with a blank face and pointed to the hole in the ground. A sick smile spread across her face. "Get in," she sang to Athena.

Athena looked down behind her and then back at Effie. "You want me to get in the hole?" She looked back at Effie. "W-was that your grave?" When she didn't answer her, Athena tried to sidestep around her as quickly as her battered body could let her. But Effie kept stepping in front of her. At least stepping is what Athena thought she was doing. She noticed now that she never really saw Effie's feet moving.

Effie stepped closer and reached her hand out, causing Athena to flinch. She tried to move away again when Effie's hand made contact with Athena's shoulder but failed as she roughly pushed her backward. Athena stumbled over the edge of the hole and instinctively tried to reach out and grab Effie, but she stepped back, avoiding her. Athena screamed as she fell back into the hole and landed on the ground with a loud thud.

Athena groaned from the impact and looked up at Effie, who just stared at her with a blank look, her head tilted to one side, studying her. She could barely see her glowing eyes peeking out from underneath her long hair. Athena tried to get up but was unsuccessful. She tried to move her right leg when a stabbing pain ran through it. Screaming from the pain, she gave up and lay on the dirt ground. She didn't want to look at her leg; she knew it was bad.

Tears flowed down her cheeks as she looked up at Effie. Effie still had that blank expression on her face, and her glowing eyes fixated on Athena. Her head wasn't tilted anymore. Slowly, her face turned into one of satisfaction as she looked down at Athena. A wicked smile spread over her face. "Please, Effie," she begged. "Don't do this." She tried to plead with the little girl standing above her, but Effie's face never changed. Never faltered.

Effie raised her hand out, and Athena heard a creaking noise above her. Her eyes widened, and the tears flowed heavier as she saw a wooden door closing opening. "No, no, no!" Athena tried to get up to stop the wooden door when another sharp pain shot through her leg. She fell back down and watched as the darkness engulfed her. She was helpless. She couldn't get up to stop Effie. She won. Her heart sank as she watched Effie's glowing, satisfied eyes disappear from her sight.

Once the door closed, she slowly sat up and felt around in the darkness. She found her phone in her back pocket. She took it out, and her heart dropped again when she felt the screen was completely shattered. Dropping it, she continued to feel around in the darkness until her hand rested on a small box. She shakily pushed against the box and breathed a sigh of relief when she figured out it was a matchbox. Her shaky hand opened the box and pulled out a match. She struck it, sending sparks flying and a soft light filling the hole. Athena held the match up to the door and looked for a way out. She tried pushing on the door, but something made it lock in place. She noticed a dozen of small holes in the wood letting in enough air for her to breathe. She got to the middle of the door and saw a lot of tick marks carved into the door and a child's writing.

It's supposed to be a punishment, but I will someday suffocate or starve in here. -Effie Richmond

Athena ran her hand over the writing. Her mouth turned down as she started feeling sad for Effie and what she must have endured here. Although, her eyes got wide when she remembered what Effie had told her.

"She really wants me to suffer as she did," she said to herself as her hand clutched at her chest. "This is how she suffered!" Athena laid back down. "I'm going to die in here. I just know it." She blew out the match and put her head in her hands. Not worrying about her dignity, she let tears flow out of her eyes and hit the ground.

"Ouch!" A piece of glass from her phone got stuck in her palm when she let her hands drop down to her side. She grabbed the piece of glass, wincing as she pulled it out of her hand.

Her phone's broken, with no one to call for help. She held onto the fact that she was to die in this hole. Not knowing what else to do, she laid down and closed her eyes, waiting for whatever will kill her to come. She had given up completely. She was defeated. Effie had won.

Athena didn't know how long she had been lying in the dark hole, but it had to be a very long time. Her stomach was growling, and her throat was parched. She opened her eyes to the sound of the wooden door opening. She covered them and groaned when a bright light flooded into the hole.

"Athena?" she heard her brother's worried voice call out for her.

"Derek?" Athena croaked.

Derek jumped down into the hole and lifted his sister into his arms. "It's okay, Athena, I've got you." He lifted her out of the hole and into someone else's arms. Athena watched as her brother heaved himself out of the hole and stood beside the man holding her. She looked up to see Mr. Schneider smiling sadly down at her.

"Good thing we found you when we did," he said to her. He carried her up the stairs and out of the basement. They walked down the long hallway and out of the door. He took her to the backseat of another car and placed her in with careful care in there.

Athena looked past him toward her car. "What about my car?" she asked them both.

Mr. Schneider closed the car door and walked to the driver's seat. Derek got into the passenger's seat and turned around to give her a supporting smile. "We will have someone come and pick it up. Don't worry, sis, we'll get you home soon." Her brother looked bad. She was sure that she looked worse, but he didn't look any better. His eyes were red and dark bags were under his eyes. His hair which used to always be neat and tidy was now messy and unkempt.

Athena returned his smile gratefully and looked out the window at the asylum. She looked up at the second-story window expecting to see the little girl standing there but did not. I guess laying in that hole helped her go through to the other side, she thought with hope to herself. She smiled with great effort and turned her attention to the two men sitting in the front seats. "How did you guys know I was in trouble?" She wrapped her arms around herself, her body growing cold.

"Derek here kept trying to call you since he hadn't heard from you," Mr. Schneider explained. He looked at her through the rearview mirror. His eyes held extreme worry as he looked over her yet again.

Derek nodded. "Yeah. I was worried." He turned around in his seat again to look at her. "You usually call me whenever you reach wherever you're going, so I assumed something happened to you when you didn't. By nature, when I couldn't get ahold of you, I called Mr. Schneider." He turned back around, his shoulders slumping. "Athena, you were gone without any communication for four days."

Four days? Athena looked out of the window watching the trees go by. Her time in there didn't feel like four days. Her body started to shiver as they drove away from the asylum. Suddenly, she remembered Ginger. She leaned forward and asked, "How's Ginger doing? Is she okay?"

Mr. Schneider looked at her again through the rearview mirror briefly before putting his eyes back on the road. "Yes, my dear. She's perfectly fine. I started to worry as well, Athena. So, we came here straight away, and when we found the hole in the floor, we both knew that you had something to do with the hole. We climbed down and found you." He glanced at her again. "Believe me, we're both glad we found you when we did."

Athena smiled and leaned her head against the window. "Thank you. Both of you." She grabbed a jacket from the seat next to her to cover herself with, let her eyes close, and fell asleep. Everything will be better now. Everything will be back to normal.

She hoped.

Athena was running down a never-ending hallway. The walls were crashing down beside her, and the floor crumbled underneath her feet. If only she could get to the door. She needed to get to the door. Her life depended on her reaching that door. But each step brought her further and further away from the door. She looked behind her and screamed as she saw Effie flying through the air toward her.

"You will pay!" Effie screamed. Her hair flowed wildly behind her, and blood came out of her mouth, spraying everywhere. Her glowing eyes had spurts of fire coming out of them. "Athena! Athena!" Her voice wasn't like how it was back at the asylum. Back there, she had a voice like a little girl, but now, her voice was deeper and hoarser. It sounded more evil than it already was. The voice almost sounded familiar to her, but she couldn't place to whom the voice belonged.

"No!" Athena screamed at her. "Stay away from me! Get away!" She turned back to run towards the door. She was so close. The door was in reach. If only she could get her hand close enough to the knob, she would be able to get out. Tears streamed down her face as she strained to reach the door. Her legs ached as she continued to run. She reached out her arm when the world started to shake without warning. She started to lose her footing as the ground beneath her shook violently. She looked down to see cracks growing underneath her feet. She stopped moving, afraid of falling through any of the cracks if she moved an inch. She looked behind her to see Effie closer than she was before. Her heart dropped as she saw how close she was to her now.

"Athena!" Effie screamed behind her. Effie was now so close that she could see the blue and purple veins threatening to pop out of her skin. Athena cringed as she looked at her.

Athena suddenly sat up with a shot in bed, causing pain to shoot through her leg. She was breathing hard and covered in sweat. Her hair stuck to her face as she sat there breathing hard. She felt a hand on her shoulder, making her jump and move away from the touch. She cried out and covered her face with her arms, trying to protect herself from whomever it was that touched her.

"Athena! Athena!" Derek sat beside her on her bed, holding his hand out. His eyes were filled with hurt and worry. If only he knew what she had been dreaming about. "It's okay. It's only me." He reached out again and waited until Athena wrapped her arms around his neck, and he hugged her back. She held onto him tightly as if she was afraid that this was all part of the dream.

Athena never wanted to let him go. If she did, she didn't know what could happen to either of them. She felt afraid. She felt as if Effie was still in the room with her, waiting for her chance to tear her apart and get her revenge. Her eyes searched the room desperately, trying to find any sign of her inside the room.

"Shh." He tried to soothe her by patting her back and petting her head. He had seen their mother do this to calm her when they were younger, but he was awkward. He never knew how to comfort her. "It's okay, I've got you. You only had a nightmare."

Athena shook her head. She tried to lean into his touch and let him comfort him the way that her mother had once comforted them both, but she didn't relax. She couldn't relax. No matter how hard she tried. She closed her eyes. "I know," she whispered. "But it looked so real." Derek sat there next to her until she calmed down and faked relaxed. She knew that he wasn't going to leave her alone until she showed that she was okay. She looked up at him and asked, "Where's Ginger?"

As if she knew they were talking about her, Ginger came running through the open door and jumped onto the bed. Ginger came and satin Athena's lap, licking her face and whining. Her butt shook back and forth. She was happy that Athena was home. Ginger started to sniff her body, looking for anything that might worry her.

Athena laughed as she tried to push her off of her. "Hi, Ginger, hi!" She continued laughing until Ginger calmed down and placed her head in her lap. "I'm happy to see you too, girl." She placed her hand on her red-furred head; a headache was starting to form and turned her attention back to Derek. "How long was I having my nightmare?"

Derek shrugged and started to pet Ginger, not looking at her. "I don't know. I've been trying to wake you up for at least five minutes." He looked up at her with worry in his eyes. "Athena, you were screaming bloody murder."

Athena looked down and pulled the covers tighter around her. The air around her was starting to get colder. She looked around the room again but didn't see any of her windows that were open. Derek must have to air on, she thought to herself. Effie couldn't be here.

The only other reason that it had gotten cold in the room was that he had turned the air on.

"What were you dreaming about?" Derek slowly asked her. His voice betrayed his fear for her. He noticed her pulling the blankets up around her and raced to get her another blanket. He came back and wrapped his around her shoulders.

She gave him a small smile as a thank you before answering him. "Effie," she whispered.

"Who?" Derek wasn't usually a patient person, but with her right now, he was. She was thankful for that.

Athena looked at her brother and fought the tears that were threatening to form and fall down her cheeks. "Effie, the girl who locked me in that hole and prevented me from leaving the asylum. I-" She looked down and bit her lip, still trying to fight the tears. She had cried too much these past couple of days and feel a slight headache forming from it. "I was running through the hallway back at the asylum, trying to get to the front door, but I never got close to it. The walls and floor were breaking and falling around me. I turned when I heard a scream behind me and saw Effie flying through the air! And- and there was blood flowing out of her mouth." She hugged her knees and rocked back and forth, letting the tears flow. The headache that was forming was getting stronger. She looked up at her brother. "I need some water."

Derek gave her a quick hug again and stood up. He reached for the glass of water sitting on her nightstand and gave it to her. "It was only a dream, sis. Whatever was in that asylum can't hurt you anymore."

She hoped he was right.

After calming herself down, Athena asked her brother to stand outside her door, so she could get ready. She didn't want him too far away in case a panic attack came. As a child; she was prone to them and knew the warning signs of one start. She was beginning to feel one start in her head. She sat in the shower letting the warm water hit her back. She covered her eyes and just cried. Her leg was hurting, but she was able to put weight onto it and limp to the bathroom. She was lucky that it wasn't broken. The headache that was forming earlier was getting worse. It was forming in the middle of her forehead, but she could feel it spreading.

She looked down at her leg, and a little cry escaped her mouth. The skin around her knee and down to her shin was covered with blue, purple, and green bruises. Her knee was swollen, and the color around her knee was darker than her shin. Athena reached out and touched it gently. She sighed relieved when she didn't feel anything out of place. It hurt like hell, but she would get through it. She needed something to help her get off of her knee for a little bit until it healed, but she'd figure that out later.

I must have just sprained it, she thought to herself. It's a bad sprain if that's what it is.

After slowly showering and getting dressed, Athena walked out of her room and met her brother outside her door. He was leaning on the other side of the hallway with his arms crossed and head down, chin touching his chest. Looking up at her with small eyes, he looked like he had just been sleeping. "There's breakfast waiting downstairs if you want any," Derek told her. He walked slowly in front of her and kept checking back to see if she needed any help. She was a little slow because of her limp, but she was able to manage. He stopped to hold out his hand so she could walk down the stairs and led her into the kitchen. A stack of waffles was waiting on the table for Athena. It had just the right amount of butter and syrup.

She smiled at her brother. "Thanks, Derek." She walked over to the plate and began to eat, her mouth watering at sight. She hadn't realized how hungry she was until she saw the large stack of waffles sitting in front of her. Derek sat down in front of her and ate his share of waffles. They made small talk while they ate and avoided any talk about the asylum. After a while, Athena got up and cleaned up the kitchen slowly; Derek kept a watchful eye on her. He knew to let her do things herself. If she needed help, she would ask him. She wasn't someone who always needed help. If she could move, she was going to do her chores herself.

He has to be exhausted, Athena thought to herself as she washed the dishes. He looked as tired as she felt. She was sure that she probably looked worse than he did.

Once the kitchen was cleaned, Athena limped over to the living room and sat on the comfy sofa, propping her leg up on the coffee table in front of her. She grabbed the remote and turned on the TV. She just wanted the extra noise. She could have sworn that she heard a little girl's voice in her head during breakfast. She couldn't tell what the voice was telling her, but she needed the noise from the TV to drown out the voice. The air around her was cold again. She turned around, pulled the blanket off the edge of the couch, and wrapped it around her shoulders. She was still shivering, even with the blanket around her. Her subconscious kept warning her that something was wrong, but she couldn't figure out what it was.

Derek carefully sat down beside her, bringing an icepack and a towel. "You should perhaps start writing your report for Mr. Schneider," Derek mentioned to her slowly as he handed her the icepack. She mumbled a thank you as she wrapped the towel around the icepack and then wrapped it around her knee, tying it in place. She didn't want to start writing the report, but she knew that she needed to. It would be good for her to make herself distracted.

Tell them everything that happened to you, a little girl's voice taunted her in her head. No one will believe you. She could have sworn that she recognized the voice that was talking in her head. She couldn't tell if that was her thinking or not. Although, her headache got worse whenever the voice popped in. She placed her hand on her forehead and pushed against it as if that would alleviate the headache.

Athena took a deep breath and waved it off. "I will come later. I just want to relax for a while." She looked over at Derek. "Please, don't push me on this," she pleaded with him. She pulled the blanket closer around her. She couldn't get warm, no matter how covered she was. She knew that it would be good for her to be done with the report so she wouldn't have to relive it, but she didn't want to think about what had happened again.

Derek nodded and grabbed her hand, giving it a small squeeze. "I won't. You need your rest. I was only reminding you." He let go of her hand and laced his hands behind his head, and watched the TV with her. They sat there in silence for a long time, just watching the tiny figures dance across the screen. She wasn't even sure what she had turned on. Eventually, she gave up trying to focus on the show and handed the remote over to Derek.

Getting bored, Athena stood up and slowly limped over to her computer. She could feel Derek's eyes watching over her while she walked. He was ready in case she fell or needed his help. She pushed the little voice out of her head and opened a tab with her email. That voice was mocking her. Not saying anything; just mocking. Even though she had just gone through all that, this was still her job. She still needed her paycheck. This was also a good distraction for her. Even as she would be writing about everything she had encountered in that asylum, writing was still a good distraction. Starting on a new email, she started her report for Mr. Schneider. Halfway through her email, she saw one corner of the screen start to turn black. It was faint at first, but then it grew and began to make its way across the whole screen.

Athena instantly stopped typing and called out to Derek. He ran over and looked at her screen.

"What the-?" he breathed. He placed a hand on the back of her chair and leaned closer next to her, trying to get a better view of what was happening.

Athena shook her head in confusion. I've got you, the voice sang in her head. What sounded like clapping echoed in her head. Athena shook her head and placed her hands on her temples to push the voice out. "What's happening, Derek? What's wrong with my computer?" She started to massage her temples.

Derek shook his head and shrugged his shoulders. "I don't know." He started to scratch the back of his head.

Athena watched helplessly as the blackness stretched toward the middle of the screen. She tried to shut off her computer, but it didn't turn off. It didn't do anything. It didn't respond to her. She slammed her hands down on each side of the computer and sighed aloud.

"I don't know what to do!" she growled. Desperate, she started to click buttons randomly. But that seemed to make the blackness spread faster.

Derek hit her shoulder. "Stop whatever you're doing!"

She spun around to face him. "Do you have any other better ideas?" You're lashing out; the singing voice appears in her head again. You're going to drive him away. No matter. He won't want to see what happens to you.

What the fuck? She placed her hands back on either side of her temples and started to rub them. A stronger headache was starting to form again in the front of her mind.

Derek flinched as if she had hit him and looked away. "No," he said quietly.

Athena turned around to find her computer screen completely black. She gasped. She watched red liquid come oozing out from her computer's sides. Derek reached from behind her and touched the red ooze with his finger. He brought it to his face and sniffed it, and then touched his tongue to it.

Athena gagged as she watched Derek. "Ew! Derek!" she exclaimed.

Derek's eyes widened. "Athena, this is blood."

Athena stood up and winced at her leg, pain shooting up her body. "Blood?" she questioned him. "Are you sure?" She looked back at her computer to see the keyboard was also covered with red ooze. Sure enough, the red darkened until it was the color and thickness of blood. "How?" she whispered. She felt her brother grab her arm and gently start pulling her back away from the computer.

All of a sudden, the blood stopped oozing out and became still. Nothing dripped from the sides, and nothing moved on the keyboard. It was as if everything was put on pause. Athena and Derek didn't move. It was as if they were in a trance and couldn't move. But, after a few seconds of dead stillness, the computer shot up and flew towards Athena and Derek. They ducked just in time to see the computer fly over their heads and shatter into the wall behind them. Athena and Derek stared wide-eyed at the shattered computer on the floor.

Now you can't write anything, a high-pitched laugh sounded in her head. Athena placed her hands on her head. Not that anyone would believe you anyway. They'll send you to an asylum just like they did to me. Another high-pitched laugh sounded in her head.

Athena opened her mouth to say something. But Derek interrupted her, asking, "You didn't take anything from that asylum when you left, did you?" His eyes were wide. He was scared, just like she was.

Athena shook her head. "No." Derek slowly helped her up off of the floor and let her lean against him. Her body was starting to feel weak. He wrapped a protective arm around her shoulders, supporting her.

Derek, still looking at the computer, sighed. "Well, I think something, or someone, followed you home."9

He's right, the voice sang. You're not going to tell him about me because he'll think you're crazy. They'll put you in an asylum just like me. The high-pitched laughter stabbed through her head.

The next two days passed excruciating slowly for Athena and Derek. Nothing unusual happened, although that just made them even more nervous. Effie was quiet in her head. Athena would look out the window every hour, hoping to see Mr. Schneider walking to the door with the Priest. Disappointment ran through her when she would never see them. Derek would pace back and forth impatiently. More than once, he threatened to go get the

Priest himself. Athena would have to calm him down and remind him to trust Mr. Schneider.

She couldn't anger Effie. She wasn't going to try to do anything that might make her snap. If the worse that she was going to do was destroy her computer, then Athena was going to leave it at that. Athena couldn't let Effie threaten them anymore, and the only way to make sure that both of them were safe as if they didn't make her mad.

"Trust him, Derek," Athena reminded him slowly when he began to pace again. "He knows what he's doing." She expected Effie to pipe up in her head, but she never did. This made Athena more nervous. She had to be plotting something. It should have made her feel better that she wasn't saying anything. That would mean that she wasn't mad, but Athena couldn't get it out of her head that something was wrong.

Derek scoffed and rolled his eyes. "If he knows what he's doing, then why is he not here?"

Athena shrugged her shoulders and looked back out the window. She was wondering the same thing. But she didn't want Derek to know she was losing faith in Mr. Schneider and his Priest. "Maybe it's hard to find a Priest to clean the house and us. Maybe if you remembered what was in that book, you could tell me why it's taking so long." Derek gave a loud sigh and stomped upstairs. Athena turned to watch him and shook her head sadly. She walked and sat down on the couch and turned on the TV. Her leg was starting to get better. Her limp wasn't as severe, but her leg was still a little swollen. The bruises were slowly turning green. Growling when the TV wouldn't turn on, she started shaking and hitting the remote against her palm, hoping it would fix it. But it didn't.

"This was working yesterday!" She threw the remote down on the couch, got up, and started to pace. Her leg was starting to heal, but it still caused her to limp. All of this stress and worry was starting to make her frustrated. She knew that Derek was getting frustrated as well, but she couldn't help him. She couldn't help herself right now. She had to wait for Mr. Schneider and his Priest. She didn't have enough patience right now.

All of a sudden, she started to feel lightheaded. She stopped walking and placed a hand on her forehead. What's wrong with me? she asked herself. She slowly walked over to the couch and sat down. She placed her head in her hands and sighed, closing her eyes when her head spun. When she tried to open her eyes and look up, her head spun even more, making her stomach churn. She bent over and placed her head between her knees.

I know what's wrong with you, Effie's voice popped into her head. Her voice was singing as she taunted Athena.

Shit. Tears started to form in her eyes. Effie was still in her head. Effie was still here. She hoped Mr. Schneider would find a Priest and come here soon. She tried to stop crying, knowing it would bring another headache, but she couldn't stop. She felt helpless.

You are helpless, Effie's laughter filled her head. You're under my control.

"Athena?" Derek asked worriedly from the staircase. "Are you okay?"

She heard his footsteps get closer and felt him sit down next to her. "I don't know. I was just walking around the house, and I got lightheaded. Now, my head is spinning, and I don't know why." Tears continued to flow down her cheeks. She didn't try to raise her head again; she didn't think that her stomach would hold its contents if she did.

I know why Effie's voice sang out. Why don't you tell him about me? Why don't you tell him that you hear my voice in your head? I have a feeling he wouldn't believe you, but he might. There was a slight pause. Why don't you have gamble? Athena could see the wicked smile that spread across Effie's face.

"Did you have breakfast this morning?" Derek's voice brought her back to the present. Distracting her from Effie's voice. He placed a hand on her shoulder and squeezed it.

Athena started to nod her head when a wave of pain shot through her head, making her stop. "Ouch! Yes, I did." Now I have another headache. Why are you doing this Effie?

I want you to suffer as I did. Effie spat at her.

I laid in that hole! Athena argued back. What more do you want?

You didn't feel pain like I did. At this moment, Effie's voice sounded small. For the first time since Athena had met her, she sounded more like the little girl that she was. Athena almost felt sorry for her.

Derek placed a hand on her shoulder. "Let me get you some pain medicine." Athena knew that pain medicine wasn't going to help. She knew that Effie was controlling her head and causing pain. She still didn't want to tell Derek about Effie's voice, but she doesn't have a choice now. She let him get the medicine in the meantime. Derek came back a few minutes later with a glass of water and a couple of pills in his hands. "Here." He placed each of them in her hands. "Take these."

Athena opened her eyes to swallow the pills and placed the glass of water on a coaster in front of her. She placed her head back in her hands. Hoping that the pills would have some effect on her, she looked around the room and smiled at Derek. "Thanks." She took a deep breath, faking that she was better. Her head was still pounding. "I think I know what's wrong with me." She started picking at her fingernails, refusing to look at him.

Wow, you're really going to tell him. Effie's laugh filled her head causing another slice of pain to go through her head. What an idiot.

Shut up!

Derek sat back down next to her and wrapped an arm around her shoulders, trying to comfort her. "Do you think it's Effie?"

Athena nodded slowly. "She never hurt me without actually touching me at the asylum. Except, maybe because she's linked to me, she can hurt me this way."

Duh. She could feel Effie roll her eyes in her head.

"I just want her to be gone," she sighed. "Derek, I can hear her in my head." Tears started to threaten to come out again.

Derek was quiet at first. "You hear her in your head?" His voice was slow and calculated.

Tears started to form in her eyes. She was starting to think of herself as a crier. She had never cried this much before. "You don't believe me." She paused. "That's fine if you don't believe me, but I'm not crazy! I hear her voice in my head. She's been communicating with me. The past two days she's been silent, but now she's speaking up again." The entire time, she kept pointing to her forehead.

Derek was quiet but squeezed her shoulders. "I believe you, sis. Why do you think she would attach herself to you?"

Athena shrugged. "She told me before she locked me in that hole that she wanted revenge and for me to feel her pain. I just heard that a couple of minutes ago in my head." She took a deep breath. "I thought she was satisfied when she locked me there, but I guess not."

"Do you know if she died in that hole?"

Athena nodded. "I have a hunch that she did - but it's just a hunch. A big one." She looked out the window, making her headache worsen from the bright light. "I'm going to lie down in bed." She got up slowly but still swayed on her feet.

"Here." Derek started to try to lift her into his arms, but Athena stopped him.

"I can walk, but just help me up there, please." Athena knew she was being stubborn, but she still wanted some sort of control over her body.

I'm surprised he believed you, Effie scoffed. That pisses me off. If you lay a hand on my brother, Athena started to threaten.

Effie started to laugh maniacally. What are you going to do, Athena? Nothing. Fucking nothing. Your brother is mine, and you'll regret making me angry.

Derek walked into Athena's bedroom a couple of hours later. He sighed thankfully and smiled at

Athena, who was still asleep in her bed. He patted her forehead gently. It was in the middle of the night, and he couldn't sleep. This whole situation unnerved him. He didn't like seeing his sister this way. He knew that she was slowly breaking, and there was no way for him to help her. He may be her younger brother, but he had promised their parents before they died that he would protect her.

He worried about her hearing Effie's voice in her head. He didn't understand how that was possible, but he wasn't about to doubt her. She had been through so much more in just over a week than she had her entire life. Derek was afraid of what could happen to her if this situation got any worse. He was worried about what could happen to him if things got worse. Effie could be attached to him for all he knew. He could end up hurting him instead of Athena.

He walked over to the window and closed the curtains. He had thought that he had closed them earlier when he had helped Athena to bed. Turning back around, he saw Athena sitting straight up in bed. He jumped in surprise. She stared straight ahead and didn't move an inch. Her eyes were wide and looked to be glazed over. She didn't even look to be breathing. She was completely still.

"Athena?" he called out to her. Slowly walking closer, he asked, "What's wrong?" He reached out to push her shoulder when her hand flashes up and grabs his wrist. He tried to pull away, but Athena wouldn't let him. He was the stronger one out of the two, but Athena's grip was like steel. Her knuckles were white with how hard she was gripping his wrist. "Athena, let me go!"

Slowly, her head turned towards him. Only her head moved; none of her body followed her. Her eyes were looking at him, but there wasn't any sign of life in them. He wasn't even sure if she was looking at him or if she was looking through him. They were glazed over. Her skin was pale and cold, slowly turning blue. When she talked, it wasn't her voice. He started to tremble. "Don't touch me," the voice growled.

"A-Athena?" Derek asked in a low tone. He took a deep breath and tried to command, "Get out of my sister, Effie." He tried to control his body and stop it from trembling.

"Athena will get what I promised to her," the voice said from within Athena's body. The voice sounded triumphant. "Your sister will be no more soon." The voice sounded like a little girl's voice. A cackle and a creepy smile grew on her face. With no warning, Athena's eyes became her own again, and the grip on Derek's wrist loosened. Athena's eyes held confusion and fear in them. She was slowly breaking, and that was breaking his own heart.

"Athena?" He grabbed her hands. They were warm again, and the color was slowly coming back to them.

Athena looked up at him. "Derek?" She started to fall back before Derek caught her. He maneuvered her, so she was sitting up against the headboard. "What happened to me?" She placed a hand on her forehead. Another headache was most likely forming again. He noticed that Effie was talking to her whenever she started to get one. He found the pattern to be rather unsettling.

Derek looked into her eyes again to make sure that she was fully back before answering. When he saw that she was fully herself again, he sighed gratefully. "You weren't yourself, Athena."

"What do you mean?" She closed her eyes and leaned her head against the headboard. Derek shook his head. "Someone was controlling you. I'm guessing whoever was controlling you was Effie. Your voice changed. It was a little girl's voice. Your skin was cold and turning blue." He held up his wrist. "You had an ice grip on my wrist." He wouldn't be surprised if bruises formed on his skin.

"Effie," she whispered. "Let me have the phone. I need to call Mr. Schneider." Derek handed her the phone, and, in a flash, she dialed Mr. Schneider's number. She rapped her fingers against her knee impatiently while she waited. When he didn't answer, she huffed and rolled her eyes. "Mr. Schneider, please call me back. It's urgent." She hung up and threw the phone on the bed. She closed her eyes once more, pinching the bridge of her nose. Derek wondered if she was talking to Effie because her eyes kept darting back and forth underneath her eyelids.

Derek looked past her towards the door and saw a shadow lingering on the wall of the hallway. That's strange, he thought. All the doors are locked. He stood up and walked cautiously over to the door.

"Derek?" Athena asked nervously. "Where are you going? Please don't go closer to the door. Come back." Her voice sounded urgent, and there was a hard warning in it, but he wasn't listening. The shadow intrigued him, and he needed to see who had entered their house.

Derek ignored her and kept walking toward the shadow. He peered out into the hallway but saw no one. The shadow, although, was still there. He stepped out into the hallway and watched as the shadow started moving. It disappeared back down the hall near the staircase. His body was telling him to stay put, but his mind wanted to see to whom that shadow belonged.

"Derek!" He heard Athena shriek behind him. He spun around to see a dark figure standing behind him with a knife in his hand. The figure was as tall as a child, and the only features Derek could see were its glowing yellow eyes. Effie.

The figure came at him with the knife. He ducked, spun it around, and pushed the figure out of the room. He slammed the door shut and locked it. Slowly, Derek backed up towards the bed and sat down beside Athena.

"Locking her out isn't going to help, Derek." Athena was trembling beside him.

Derek gave her a sharp look. "What was I supposed to do? Let her stab me?" He watched as Athena squeezed her eyes shut and covered her ears. Her eyes were darting back and forth beneath her eyelids. He started to reach out for her when a knife flew through the door and landed in Derek's arm.

He screamed in surprise and pain and grabbed the hilt of the knife. Athena tried to stop him, but he pulled it out quickly. A green ooze started falling down the knife and mixed with his blood. He didn't know what the green ooze was, but it started to make him feel weird and weak. He started to sway back and forth before falling back onto the bed.

"Derek?" he heard Athena's worried voice call out to him. His vision started to blur and darken. He tried to reach out for his sister but in a matter of seconds, he couldn't see anything at all. And he blacked out.

Athena looked at her unconscious brother lying on her bed with worry. She cautiously picked up the knife that had struck him and looked at the green ooze still dripping off it. She knew that Effie was to blame for this. She knew that the shadow Derek had pushed out of her room was Effie. She could hear her laughing the entire time in her head. She suspected that the green ooze on the handle and coming out of Derek's arm had to be a poison of some sort.

So smart, Athena. Effie laughed in her head.

But why? Athena questioned her. What had Derek done to make you mad? You should only be attacking me, not Derek. All that Athena had done to Effie was go into that asylum. Although, if Effie had been waiting for her revenger for who knows how long, Athena was the closest and only person whom she could latch onto.

She dropped the knife onto her bed and raced into the bathroom, grabbing some towels and racing back towards her brother. Effie was silent in her head. She never answered her questions. She knelt beside Derek and began to clean the knife wound. She cleaned it the best she could before wrapping a towel tightly around it, hoping to stop the bleeding. She had never had to do any of this before, but she had watched plenty of crime shows and tried to mimic what they were doing.

The phone started to ring on the bed beside her. In haste, she grabbed the phone and clicked the accept button. She brought the phone up to her ear and panted out, "Hello?"

"Miss Athena?" the voice said from the other side of the phone. "It's Mr. Schneider."

Athena sighed thankfully. "Oh, thank goodness! Mr. Schneider, we need that Priest now! Effie just tried to kill Derek, and I'm afraid she's not done with me." Athena began breathing hard again, and beads of sweat started to form on her forehead. It felt like the room had turned into a sauna.

"I know, honey. I have the Priest, and we'll be at your house soon." There was a pause before he continued, "Just try to stay alive."

Athena let out a desperate chuckle. "How soon?" The panic in her voice was obvious.

"In about an hour." Mr. Schneider paused before continuing. "Hang in there." He hung up, making Athena take the phone away from her ear and throw it on her bed.

She looked down at her unconscious brother in front of her. She needed to go downstairs and be ready for Mr. Schneider, but she didn't want to leave Derek. She looked around the room for a while and sighed. She leaned her back against the headboard and stayed with him. Tears formed in her eyes again.

Just hurt me, she pleaded. Just hurt me.

This is hurting you. Effie finally spoke up in her head. You and your brother are close. Hurting him means that I'm hurting you.

What did you do to him? What is that ooze?

It was like she could feel Effie shrugging her shoulders in her mind. Something I created. I don't know whether I want to wake him up yet or not, Athena.

Athena closed her eyes as the tears flowed even faster down her cheeks. She sat like that for an hour until she heard the front doorbell ring. The ring sounded foreign and unnaturally loud in the quiet, eerie house. Athena reluctantly got off of the bed and gave her brother a quick kiss on his forehead. "I'll be right back, Derek." She hurried down the stairs and opened the front door, letting in Mr. Schneider and the Priest.

Mr. Schneider quickly embraced Athena and introduced her to the Priest standing behind him. "This is Father Calvin. Father, this is the woman I told you about."

The tall, greying Priest held out his hand and Athena shook it. "It's nice to meet you, Athena. I can already feel the bad energy radiating throughout your house. I can feel the spirit's presence on you just touching your hand." He turned and started to walk around the house. He held on tightly to the Bible at his side. Athena and Mr. Schneider followed him.

Athena started to grow even more nervous as the long minutes passed by. She could feel her heart beating violently inside her chest. It began beating so hard she thought that it would jump right out. She wrung her hands together repeatedly. She was surprised at how quiet Effie was in her head.

What if Father Calvin couldn't get the spirit out of her house? Would she have to move away? Would Effie follow wherever Athena and Derek went? Hundreds of questions filled her mind as she followed Father Calvin up the stairs and through all the rooms. She waited for Effie to sarcastically answer all of her questions, but there wasn't a single noise from her.

When they reached Athena's bedroom, she expected Derek to still be lying on the bed, but he was gone. She gasped and started to shake. "Where's Derek?"

Father Calvin turned around and gave her a confused look. "Who?"

"My brother," Athena explained quickly. "Derek." She pointed to the bed where a small pool of blood and ooze was still on her bedspread. "I left him laying right there. The spirit, Effie, threw a knife and hit Derek on his arm. He passed out, and I left him here when you both came to the door." Walking over to the bed, she searched for the knife. Finding it underneath a pillow, she brought it over to Father Calvin. "This was the knife that she threw." Holding it up, green ooze started falling down it again.

Father Calvin took the knife gently in his hands and inspected it. "What is this green goo?"

Athena shrugged her shoulders. "I don't know, Father. Effie told me that she was the one who made it, and it caused Derek to pass out. He never faints at the sight of blood."

Father Calving looked up at her. "You can talk to the spirit?"

Athena bit her lip as she nodded. "Yes, I can hear her in my head." She waited a couple of seconds for Effie's voice again but didn't hear her. "I can't hear her now."

Father Calvin nodded as he started to touch the green ooze. The door to Athena's bathroom started too slowly open. They all turned to look, just to see Derek standing at the bathroom door. He didn't look like himself. His smile was gone and replaced by a thin line. His eyes were glazed over and not looking at anyone.

"Derek?" Athena called out to him. She started to race towards him, but Father Calvin grabbed her arm, holding her back. "Snap out of it, Derek!" She looked down at his hands. She saw a large, sharp shard of glass and blood running down his hand. Blood was dripping onto the floor. "Don't do it, Derek." She finally understood why Effie was quiet. "Effie, let him go!"

Derek stared at them emotionless, the bloody glass shard still in his hand. Athena tried talking to him - tried talking to Effie - but she could tell that he couldn't hear her. She turned to Father Calvin, frantic, who was staring at Derek.

"Can you help him?" she asked him, her voice trembling.

Father Calvin reached inside his jacket and pulled out a cross on a chain. "Get behind me, Athena. No matter what happens, you need to remember that he is not your brother." Athena started to open her mouth to argue with him, but he interrupted her. "Whatever spirit lurks in this house has attached itself to him." He held the cross out in front of himself. He started to mutter phrases in Latin under his breath.

Athena looked at Derek and frowned as she saw no change in him. "Whatever you're doing isn't working!" She was growing impatient. Effie, you better let go of him soon, she tried to reach Effie, but there was no response.

Mr. Schneider grabbed her hand and pulled her towards him. "Shush, Athena. Let Father Calvin do his work."

Athena shut her mouth and watched Derek. He stared with a blank face at Father Calvin. His grip on the glass shard grew tighter, causing a stream of blood to flow down his hand and drip onto the floor.

Father Calvin closed his eyes and continued to mutter his phrases under his breath. The cross hanging from the chain started to move in little circles.

"Come out of Derek, spirit, and leave this family alone!" Father Calvin finally said aloud with a commanding voice.

Effie made Derek throw his head back and laugh. "You think you can scare me with that form of method?" Effie's little jesting voice came out of Derek's mouth. "How dumb do you think I am?" He held up the glass shard and pointed to Athena. "I am not done with that wretched girl yet. I told you that you would feel my pain!" He threw the shard, making Athena and Mr. Schneider jump out of the way.

Mr. Schneider fell into the hallway, and the door shut on him, leaving him separated from everyone else. Athena jumped into a desk and unintentionally pushed a picture frame off of it. The picture frame fell onto the floor and shattered. Athena looked up at the wall and saw the bloody shard sticking out of the wall. She felt her head being yanked back by a strong hand, and flung her across the room.

She crashed into the wall and grimaced at the sudden pain flowing through her body. Looking up, she saw Derek stalking toward her.

"Derek," Athena whispered as she held up a bloody hand. "Please, don't do this." She could hear Mr. Schneider pounding on the other side of the door, screaming to be let back in. He was pleading with Effie.

Father Calvin was quick to step in between Athena and Derek. He raised the cross again. This time, he was more forceful in his words, "Come out of Derek, spirit. Leave this family and house alone!"

Derek stopped and held his arm out behind him towards the glass shard that was still lodged in the wall. It came flying towards his hand, and he grabbed it, causing fresh blood to drip down his hand again. Derek smiled diabolically at Father Calvin. His eyes did not meet his smile; they were still glassed over.

"This is what you get for getting in my way," he sneered. "I warned you. I will have her pay." He threw the shard at Father Calvin as Athena screamed. The shard lodged itself in his stomach, but it didn't stop. The force of the throw caused the shard to come out through his back and hit the wall above Athena's head, barely missing her.

Father Calvin slowly looked down at the hole created in his stomach. The cross slowly fell out of his hand and landed on the floor. His knees buckled, and he fell with a thud onto the floor.

Athena crawled over to him and rolled him over so he was on his back. "Father Calvin!" Tears flowed from her eyes as she watched his blood flow out of his body and onto her floor. She started to put shaking hands on the hole, but she knew it wasn't going to make a difference.

He reached out to the cross with shaky hands, putting it into her hand. "Finish the job." His voice was grave.

Athena looked down at the cross. "But I don't know how to get a spirit out of someone!"

"Just touch him with this." He motioned to the cross still clutched in her hand. His eyes went back to his head as he took his last, shaky breath.

Athena looked up at Derek, who laughed and shook his head. She had heard that laugh too often in her head in the past few days. She needed to take care of this, and she needed to do it now. Slowly, she stood up and faced him. Blood stained her clothes. Whether it was hers or Father Calvin's, she didn't know. All she knew was that she had to save her brother.

She held out the cross in front of her and readied her stance. Glaring at her brother, she said, "Come and get me, Effie."

Derek stopped laughing and stared at Athena. Both of them stared at each other for a while, not moving a muscle. She still held out the cross in front of her. Finally, Derek made the first move. He charged at her with supernatural speed, but Athena was quicker. Full of adrenaline, she pressed the cross into Derek's forehead when he was an arm's length away.

A burning sensation started to appear on Derek's face. The smell of burnt flesh filled the air. A little girl's scream shrieked out of Derek's mouth. He clawed at Athena's hand, drawing blood.

Hissing, Athena let go and was surprised to see the cross was still stuck to Derek's face. Derek still worked to claw and pull the cross off his face, but it wouldn't budge. He thrashed around the room until he fell onto the floor and screamed. Athena covered her ears as the scream pierced her ears and lasted for a full minute before he became silent and limp. The cross fell off his face and onto the floor.

Everything became silent.

Athena watched with a heart full of hope as Derek slowly sat up. She hesitated to rush towards him as she watched him rub his head and the back of his neck. The imprint of the cross on his forehead was gone, and the light in his eyes was finally back. He was starting to return to himself again. When he finally looked over at Athena, his eyes started to water, and his mouth turned down.

"Athena?" he croaked.

Athena finally knew that her brother was back. She rushed over and embraced him.

"Is she gone?" Derek asked her in a timid voice. "I can't hear her in my head anymore."

Athena nodded quickly. "Yes. Oh, Derek, I'm so happy you're back!" She knew she was going to have a headache with how much she was letting herself cry.

Derek hugged his sister tighter and looked over her shoulder. He pushed away from her and moved back as his eyes widened. She followed his eyes to where Father Calvin's body was lying a few feet away from them in a pool of blood. His body shook as he couldn't take his eyes off of body.

"Please tell me that I didn't do that," his voice shook and cracked.

Athena looked over at Father Calvin's body again, shuttered, and then back at her brother. "Derek," she started slowly. "Effie was in control of you. You didn't do it, okay? She did."

Derek's shoulders were still stiff as he looked back at Athena. "She still used my body to commit it, Athena."

Athena opened her mouth to try to argue with him when the bedroom door swung open. Mr. Schneider ran through the open door and stopped short at sight in front of him.

His eyes widened more at the sight of Father Calvin and the pool of blood around him. He then looked over at Athena and Derek. Seeing that Derek was back to his usual self, his eyes softened. He quickly walked over to the two young people and wrapped them up in a large hug.

"I'm so glad you both are safe," he breathed a sigh of relief. "Come on." He helped them up. "I called the police and paramedics; they should be here soon. Let's go meet them."

Athena tugged lightly on Mr. Schneider's hand. "How are we going to explain everything that happened?"

Mr. Schneider looked back at her and gave her a reassuring look. "I'll handle everything." Athena had no choice but to believe him.

----------------------------

The next few weeks went by in a blur for Athena. After the entire house was cleaned and Father Calvin's body was taken away, another Priest came into Athena's house. He finished cleaning the rest of Effie's spirit out of her house. She hadn't heard her voice in weeks. No scary laughter filled her head anymore. Her leg hadn't given her any problems after a week. She doesn't walk with a limp anymore, although bruises still cover her body.

Athena had nightmares after that day's events. She would wake up in the middle of the night drenched with sweat. Her dog would move and lay her head on Athena's lap, trying to comfort her. But after a few days, the nightmares stopped and was able to get a full night's sleep.

After Effie had broken her old one, Mr. Schneider got her a get-well computer. Athena finally used this new computer to finish her report on the Sarton Asylumish her report on the Sarton Asylum. The report was a big hit, rewarding both her and Mr. Schneider a lot of money. She believes it was a big hit because of the news report. There were reporters outside her house for a couple of days before Mr. Schneider was able to get them to move on.

Athena woke up one bright morning and stretched in bed. She got out slowly and walked over to her window. Opening the window, she leaned out and breathed in the fresh air. She has learned to appreciate everything about every day. She heard the soft roar of a car driving down her driveway.

"Ginger!" she yelled excitedly to her dog. "Derek's here!"

Ginger barked and jumped off the bed. Athena chased after her dog out of the room and down the stairs. She opened the front door, smiling at Derek as he got out of the car and walked towards her. She was very thankful that the cross hadn't left a permanent mark on his forehead. He had started to go to a therapist that Mr. Schneider had connected him too. He was still working through much of what had happened to him, but he was slowly improving.

"How are you feeling?" she asked him.

Derek laughed. "Like every morning you have asked that question, I feel fine." He hugged her and walked inside, brushing Ginger's head as he passed her.

Athena led him into the kitchen, took a toaster from a cabinet, and placed it on the counter. "What do you want to eat for breakfast? I'm wanting toast."

Derek shrugged as he sat down at the table. "I already ate." Athena turned around to give him a skeptical look. "Honest, sis, I did!" He gave her a convincing smile before she turned back around. Athena place two pieces of bread into the toaster and turned it on. "I do have some news for you," Derek announced.

"Oh?" Athena turned around and leaned against the counter. "What is this news?"

Derek reached into his pants pocket and pulled out a folded piece of paper. "It's from Mr. Schneider." He handed the paper to Athena. "There is no pressure to accept this, sis. He just thought you'd like to do something."

Athena smiled and took the piece of paper from him. "Where would I be going?" She started to unfold the paper.

Derek leaned back in his chair. "Another asylum, but this time in Italy." He pointed the finger at her. "And this time I'm coming with you. First of all, it's in Italy. Second of all, I'm not letting you out of my sight."

Athena smiled and thought about this offer for a while. There was a large chance that they could go through another situation with another spirit like Effie. They would have to go through that whole experience again, but then again, there might not be. Her curiosity was getting the best of her, and she cursed at herself as she looked up at her brother and nodded. After all, she liked the adventure and the danger that came from it.

"Let's go."

**The End**

# OTHER BOOKS BY THE AUTHOR

Karmic Love

Undercover

Eternal Love

Undying Lust

The Good Taste

Offence and Justice

A Model for Murder

Lethal Legacy

Lethal Legacy 2

Paranormal Club

Enchanted Souls

Beginners of Nowhere

Wildflower

Mystic Agent

Dark Angel

Lonesome Moonlight

# SIR PATRICK BIJOU

The Eerie Egg

A Romantic Crime .

Passionate Alien

The Critical Case

In the Shadow

Mental Asylum

www.ingramcontent.com/pod-product-compliance
Lightning Source LLC
Chambersburg PA
CBHW070510170726
48291CB00008B/2698